Maybe today Carrie would come home...

"Carrie."

Every time I said her name, part of it stuck in my throat.

"She's going to come home, Amy. I know it. And I have to be here when she does."

"It's been five months, Mom," I said. "When are you going to stop waiting for Carrie?"

"Never!" She spun around so fast that she almost lost her balance. "I'll wait for five months, five years. It doesn't matter. I'll never stop waiting. She's my daughter!"

"So am I!"

What about me? Don't I count? Carrie's the one who ran away—so why am I the one who is being punished?

MISSING:
Carrie Phillips, Age 15

by Janet Dagon

For David—
my husband and best friend

Published by Worthington Press
7099 Huntley Road, Worthington, Ohio 43085

Printed in the United States of America
10 9 8 7 6 5 4 3

ISBN 0-87406-421-x

Part 1

The Last Days of October

One

"**A**MY, you have to go to Sarah's party to-night, you just *have* to," my friend Lisa pleaded over the phone. "Everyone's going to be there. Marsha Wilson, David Murdock..."

I walked from one end of the kitchen to the other while Lisa rattled off the names of everyone I knew. "I don't know, Lis," I said when she was finished. "I'll have to think about it."

"Come on, Amy. It can't be that bad."

The *it* Lisa was referring to was the perm I'd gotten the night before. For months I'd been aching for a new look. So, when Sarah Jenkins invited our entire class to the country club for her 13th birthday party, I'd decided it was the perfect time to launch the "new" me. "I'd like something short and sassy," I'd told the girl at Henrietta's Hair Emporium. She winked and blinked and nodded, and I'd thought she understood. But two hours later, I walked out with a head full of frizz.

"You haven't seen it, Lis," I said, twisting the telephone cord around my finger.

"Maybe it would look better if you washed it," Lisa suggested.

"I tried that this morning. I washed it and blew it dry and brushed it. Now I look like a used Brillo Pad."

"It's too bad it isn't a costume party."

That's cute, Lis—real cute, I thought.

We talked for another 15 minutes. Actually, Lisa talked, and I listened. She told me about the dress she was going to wear and how she was going to fix her hair, and how the band Sarah's parents had hired was the absolute best because she had heard them at her cousin's wedding. I oohed and ahhed in all the right places. But when I hung up the phone, I wanted to cry.

Sarah's party was going to be *the* social event of the entire year—maybe *the* social event of my entire life. And I was afraid to go. I was afraid to show my face. I was afraid they'd all laugh at me.

The most important night of your life, and you blew it. Face it, Phillips. You're a loser.

I walked through the dining room and into the living room where Mom and Dad were busy painting—turning perfectly good white walls to the color of mustard. All the furniture had been shoved to one side and covered with drop cloths. The floor was a jumble of old sheets and bedspreads and yards of some kind of plastic Dad had found in the garage.

I circled around everything, looking for a place to land. "My life is totally ruined," I said, sinking to a spot in the middle of the floor.

"I told you not to wash it," Mom said as she dipped her brush into the paint.

"It doesn't make any difference," I said, touching my hair. It felt like cotton candy. "I couldn't have gone to the party looking the way I did before I washed it, either."

"You're making a big mistake, Amy. You may never get a chance to see the inside of the country club again."

"The country club!" Dad's voice fell from the top of the ladder he was standing on. "Who's going to the country club?"

Mom sighed. "Peter, don't you ever listen to what's going on around here?" He gave her a blank look as she continued, "Sarah Jenkins is having a birthday party at the country club tonight, and Amy was invited."

"It's at the country club," he repeated.

"Yes, Peter, the birthday party is at the

country club," Mom said again.

"Yeah, Dad, it's at the country club," I added, looking for a little sympathy, but he didn't seem to hear.

"Since when do the Jenkinses belong to the country club?" he asked.

"They've been members ever since they won the state lottery," Mom said.

"Oh, yeah, I forgot about that."

Mom rolled her eyes and shook her head, and I knew exactly what she meant. How could anyone forget that someone in our town had won 10 million dollars?

"I guess I'll have to start buying lottery tickets again," Dad said, rolling a strip of yellow paint on to the wall.

"And what would you do if you won?" Mom asked.

"I'd retire. I'd spend the rest of my life playing golf, and I'd *hire* someone to paint the living room."

Mom knelt on the floor and jabbed her brush into the corner. "Bill Jenkins didn't retire. He still works for the sanitation department."

"You're kidding!" Dad's roller stopped in the middle of a roll. "Why doesn't he quit?"

Mom shrugged. "I guess he likes his work."

"He likes collecting garbage?"

They rambled on and on, trying to decide what Mr. Jenkins should and shouldn't do with the rest of his life, while *my* life was falling apart. And they didn't even care.

There was a paint can a few inches from my foot. If I knocked it over, would they notice? I stretched my leg and was tapping the tip of my sneaker on the side of the can when I heard my sister, Carrie, coming down the stairs. I turned and looked and knew the minute I saw her that I'd been wasting my time talking to Mom and Dad. Carrie's the one I should've gone to.

She was two years older than me and a zillion times smarter—not book smarter—life smarter. Nothing ever confused her. She always knew what she wanted, and she never let someone else's opinion get in her way. She just didn't care what anyone else thought—and if I'd asked her about the party, she would've talked me into going.

But I didn't ask her. I couldn't. I wasn't talking to her.

Two nights ago, I caught her rummaging through my dresser drawer—the one where I keep all my baby-sitting money—and I yelled and screamed and called her all kinds of names, until Mom came in and grounded me. She grounded *me*! I swore right then and there that I'd never talk to Carrie again.

So, I just sat there, in the middle of the floor, tapping my foot on the side of the paint can, and watched her leave. Her jeans were too long, her sweatshirt too short, and the straps on her backpack were so frayed that they looked like they'd break any minute.

"Supper's at six. Don't be late!" Mom yelled from behind me.

Carrie didn't answer. She didn't even look our way. She just opened the door and left.

Two

IT took four hours, three shampoos, a bottle of conditioner, a can of mousse, and a curling iron for me to realize the perm wasn't going to go away. *If only I could go back in time 24 hours, slip into yesterday, know then what I know now*, I thought. *If I was in charge of the world, I'd let people do that. A 24-hour time exchange would make things so much easier.*

I opened the top drawer of my dresser, swept all the combs and brushes in, slammed the drawer shut, and went downstairs for supper.

Except for the mustard-colored walls, the living room was back to normal. I went into the kitchen. The table was set, but no one was around. The door to the basement was open, and I could hear Dad down there, mumbling something about women always changing their minds. From the window, I saw Mom outside, flipping burgers on the gas grill. She was wearing Dad's old windbreaker and had to keep pushing up the sleeves every time she moved the spatula.

I walked outside. The cold October air caught me off guard and I rubbed my arms to take away the chill. "Mom, I don't know what to do about the party tonight."

"Amy, if you want to go to the party, go. If you don't want to go, then don't go." She slapped slices of cheese on the burgers and slammed the lid of the grill. "I hate the color of the living room, and your father refuses to paint it again. He won't even listen—" She turned toward me and flinched. "What did you do to your hair?"

"I washed it."

"Again?"

I actually had washed it three times, but I didn't tell her that. I just nodded and tried to swallow the lump in my throat. If only she'd tell me it didn't look *that* bad. If only she'd offer to help. But she just stood there, shaking her head, her face squeezed into a lump of disgust. Giant puffs of smoke were sneaking out of the grill. She lifted the lid.

"These are almost ready," she said, nudging the burgers away from the flames. "Did

Carrie come home yet?"

I shrugged. "I don't know. I guess so. The table's set."

"I set the table," Mom said.

"I thought it was Carrie's turn."

"It was, but she must have forgotten."

"How come *she* always forgets, and *I'm* the one you call irresponsible? Why do you always stick up for *her*?"

"I don't."

"Yes, you do." Mom's shoulders stiffened, and I knew I was headed for trouble. But the party was only two hours away. My hair was a wreck. And I was miserable. "You're always making excuses for her, like 'Carrie must've forgotten,' or 'Carrie must've misunderstood,' or 'Carrie probably didn't hear me.'"

"Amy..."

"Even when I caught her snooping around in my room, you grounded *me*!"

"You're the one who was screaming like a maniac."

"But she—"

"That's enough! One more word, and you won't have to decide about that party. You'll be grounded again!"

I bit my lip.

She took a deep breath, and when she let it out, her shoulders sagged. "Now, go call

13

Melonie's house, and tell Carrie to come home for supper."

I stomped inside and called Carrie's friend, but Carrie wasn't there.

Mom came inside with the burgers. "Did you call her?" she asked as she set the plate on the table.

"Yeah, but she wasn't there."

She took off the windbreaker, hung it on a hook next to the basement door, and called Dad. "Peter, supper is ready."

I sat at the table and stared at the food. The burgers were burned around the edges, and the cheese was covered with a smoky haze. They looked as lousy as I did.

As soon as Dad appeared, Mom started complaining about how the color of the paint in the living room was all wrong, how it clashed with everything, and how maybe—just maybe—they could try wallpaper.

"Can't we just leave it alone for a while?" Dad asked as he sat down. "Maybe it'll start to grow on you. You may even end up liking it."

Never, I thought.

"Never," Mom said.

Dad sighed and reached for a hamburger roll. "Where's Carrie?"

"I don't know." Mom glanced at the clock

and then looked at me. "Did Melonie say what time Carrie left?"

"She didn't leave."

"You said she did."

"No, I didn't. I said she wasn't there."

"Amy, don't play games with me."

"I'm not. Melonie's mom answered the phone, and she said Carrie wasn't there."

"Then she must have gone somewhere with Melonie."

"Nope. Melonie has some kind of stomach virus. She's been barfing her guts up all day."

Dad groaned.

Mom turned a funny shade of green. "We're trying to eat."

Sorry, I said to myself.

I promised myself I wouldn't cry. After all, there would be other parties. *Wouldn't there?* And this wasn't the end of the world. *Was it?* And I had learned a valuable lesson. *Hadn't I? So, there was absolutely no reason to be upset.*

But at eight o'clock, I was locked in my room, crying my heart out.

A little while later, Mom knocked on my door, "Amy?" I thought she had come to comfort me, to wrap me in her arms like she had when I was little, and to tell me everything would be okay. But she hadn't.

"Do you have any idea where Carrie is?" she asked when I opened the door.

"No."

"Are you sure?"

"Yes."

"Positive?"

"Yes!"

"She's not home yet." Her voice was flat, and she had a funny kind of look in her eyes, as if she was trying to see something that wasn't there. "I'm going to call Melonie's house again. What's her number?"

"It's 555-5234."

She left, and I stood there, watching her go down the stairs. Then I kicked the door shut and fell on my bed.

It was almost nine o'clock when Mom called me again. I picked myself off the bed and went into the hall to see what she wanted.

She was standing at the bottom of the stairs. "Go get Carrie's address book out of her room, and bring it down for me."

"Isn't she home yet?"

"No, and I'm going to call every person she knows until I find her."

Walking into Carrie's room was like going through a time tunnel. Her walls were covered with posters, but they weren't the posters a normal kid her age would have had. These were black and white blow-ups of Humphrey Bogart, Clark Gable, Greer Garson, and Katharine Hepburn. I knew they were old movie stars because she told me. Carrie had this thing for the past.

I walked over to her bed and picked up her Raggedy Ann doll. We both had one. Mine was in a box on the top shelf of my closet, but Carrie never put hers away. Every time her friends saw it, they laughed, but she didn't care. That was the one great thing about her—she just didn't care.

I sat on the bed and hugged the doll. *Carrie would have gone to the party. It wouldn't have mattered if she was bald. If she wanted to go, she would have gone, even if everyone had laughed.*

"Amy, did you find it?" Mom yelled from downstairs. I jumped off the bed and ran to Carrie's desk. "I'm still looking." It took a few minutes, but I found it under a pile of old test papers in the bottom drawer. The cover was ripped, and some of the pages were stuck together. I knew Mom wasn't going to find any current phone numbers in it.

Carrie didn't write them down anymore. She didn't have to. They were all in her head.

I shut the drawer and started to turn off the light. And that's when I noticed it. The football jersey—it was gone.

Six months ago, when we were cleaning the attic, Carrie found Dad's old high school football jersey. It was scarlet with a gray 36 plastered on its back. For some reason she went crazy over it, so Dad gave it to her. And she had slept in it every night since then. During the day, it hung on her doorknob—but it wasn't there now. I looked in her closet, under her bed, and went through her dresser drawers, but I couldn't find it.

She wouldn't have let anyone borrow it, and she never wore it outside the house. It was something sacred—I could tell by the way she hugged it every time it came back from being washed.

The jersey was gone.

Carrie was gone.

And somewhere deep inside, I knew she wasn't coming back.

Three

I tried to tell my parents about the football jersey, but they wouldn't listen. After Dad drove around town looking for Carrie and Mom dialed every number in Carrie's address book, they called the police.

"But you don't understand," Mom said to the policeman who was sitting in our recliner at 11:00 that night. "Carrie never left the house *without* her backpack. She was always trading records and books with her friends and then hauling them back to trade some more." She let out a short, nervous laugh. "Why I bet half the things in her room right now aren't really hers. Right, Amy?"

I just nodded and stared at the uniformed stranger who was sunk in everyone's favorite chair as if he belonged there. He was a huge man with fingers the size of sausages, and a forehead that ended at the top of his skull.

His hair must have been transplanted to his eyebrows. They were like two overgrown bushes drooping over slate gray eyes. Every few minutes I looked for Carrie, wanting to share that split-second eye contact that told me she was thinking the same thing.

But she wasn't there.

Mom started babbling about what a good girl Carrie was. If she hadn't mentioned her by name, I wouldn't have known who she was talking about. It's not that Carrie is really bad—she isn't. But Mom was making her sound like some kind of saint, and she isn't that, either.

The man with the eyebrows cut her off in mid-sentence. "The way I see it, Mr. and Mrs. Phillips, your daughter has either run away from home or she has friends you don't know about."

"No, you're wrong," Mom said, as she swung her head toward Dad. "Peter, tell him. Make him understand that something terrrible has happened to Carrie."

Dad was sitting on the deacon's bench, looking like something out of a horror movie—wide-eyed, pasty, and silent.

"Amy." Mom swung toward me. Her face was like a piece of crumbled tissue paper. "Tell him. Tell him Carrie wouldn't run away.

Tell him she had no secrets."

Everyone has secrets, Mom, I thought. But Eyebrows didn't give me a chance to answer.

"Mrs. Phillips," he said, hoisting himself out of his seat, "I realize how upsetting this is to you and Mr. Phillips."

Hey, what about me? I felt like yelling.

"But there's nothing we can do until your daughter's been missing for 24 hours."

Dad shot off the bench. "You're not going to do anything for 24 hours?"

"No, sir."

"Then why did you even bother coming?"

"Your wife reported a kidnapping, Mr. Phillips. And if there was any evidence to support that theory, we would certainly take action."

"Evidence!" Mom jumped to her feet. "What kind of evidence do you want? She said she was going to her girl friend's house, and she never got there."

"No, she didn't," I said. They all looked at me as if I'd just fallen from the sky. "She didn't say where she was going. We just *thought* she was going to Melonie's house, because that's where she usually goes on Saturday afternoons."

"No, Amy, you're wrong," Mom said, and then she turned to Eyebrows. "Amy was upset

21

all afternoon about a party she was supposed to go to tonight. She wasn't paying attention when Carrie left. She didn't hear her."

I looked at the door, and I could still see Carrie standing there, her hand on the knob, and her backpack hanging on one shoulder. But I couldn't see her face, I couldn't see what she was saying.

No, Mom, you're the one who's wrong. Carrie left, and no one asked her where she was going, I thought.

Mom and Dad stayed up all night.

I lay in bed, staring at a patch of moonlight on my ceiling and listening. I listened to the sound of water running on my ceiling, the tea kettle whistling, footsteps pacing the floor, and the silence from Carrie's room.

I listened until I couldn't listen anymore.

Four

"I told you, didn't I? Didn't I tell you?" It was Sunday morning, and we were standing in the hall right outside my room. Mom's eyes were so red and swollen that they looked like blisters.

"But why would she?" Mom asked. "Why would Carrie run away?"

I didn't have the answer to that question, and I was too angry to think of one, but at least Mom finally believed me.

She had to believe me. There were too many things missing—my earrings that were mother-of-pearl with 14-carat gold stems. They had been a birthday present from my parents, and they were the only earrings I had that weren't 99¢ specials from the discount store. *Gone.*

My baby-sitting money, which was 35 dollars, had been snatched from my dresser drawer that Carrie had been snooping in when *I* got grounded. *Gone.*

Mom's favorite gold chain, the one Dad gave her for their 10th anniversary, the one she kept in a velvet-lined box so it wouldn't get tangled with all her other stuff. *Gone.*

Fifty dollars in ones and fives that had been stashed away for my allergy shots. *Gone.*

Carrie left because she wanted to. Carrie always did what she wanted to, and somehow she always got away with it. But she never did anything like this before.

"Why?" Mom asked again. "Why, why, why?" The front door slammed, and we both jumped.

"Elizabeth?" Dad called.

"I'm up here," Mom answered. "What did the police say?" she asked as Dad walked up the stairs into the hallway.

"We can file a missing person's report," Dad said. His face was flushed and damp. "They need a recent picture of Carrie. That's what I came back for."

"I'll go get the one I have in my wallet," Mom said. She brushed past me and walked down the hall to their room.

Dad leaned against the wall. Everything about him seemed to sag as if his skin was falling off his bones. "I never thought some-

24

thing like this would happen to us," he said, more to himself than to me. "Other people have these problems, not us."

* * * * *

It's funny how when one thing happens, it can make you forget about something else. I had forgotten about the party until Lisa called me that afternoon.

"Amy, where were you last night? You missed the whole thing!"

I slid down the kitchen wall and plopped on the floor. "I told you I didn't think I'd be able to make it."

"But you missed it! You missed everything!"

I held the phone between my head and shoulder and rubbed my thighs. "It was that great, huh?"

"Great? It was a disaster!"

My head shot up, and the phone crashed to the floor. "Lis, are you still there?" I asked when I picked up the receiver.

"You dropped me!"

"I'm sorry. So, tell me what happened at the party."

"There was a food fight. It was the biggest, ugliest, messiest food fight you've ever seen."

"It happened at the country club?"

"Yep. Amy, it was unbelievable. One minute I was standing there talking to Marsha Wilson, and the next minute—whamm-o! I was covered with spaghetti."

They served spaghetti? I wondered. I don't know what I was expecting from the country club, but it wasn't spaghetti. "They actually served spaghetti?"

"Well, not exactly," Lisa explained. "Sarah loves Italian food, so her dad ordered a bunch of pasta. I guess it was fettucini, or maybe it was linguini. I don't know. It all looks like spaghetti to me."

"So, who started the fight?"

I never heard the answer. Mom came out of nowhere and snatched the phone from my hand. "Mo-om!" I protested.

"Lisa," she said into the receiver, "this is Mrs. Phillips. You will have to talk to Amy another time. I'm waiting for a very important phone call." Then she rolled her eyes and said, "No, she can't call you back later. She'll see you tomorrow in school." And then she hung up.

"Mom, how could you?"

"You can't sit around here all day tying up the phone."

"All day?" I jumped up so fast, I almost lost my balance. "I wasn't even on the phone five

26

minutes. All you had to do was ask, and I could've told you that."

She laughed. But it wasn't her ha-ha-that's-funny laugh, but her ha-ha-you-have-got-to-be-kidding laugh that she saved for special moments like this.

"Aw, come on, Mom. You could've at least given me a warning."

"There isn't any time for warnings. What if Carrie was trying to call or the police, and the line was busy?"

So, she or they would've called back, I thought. It was one of those answers that seemed to make a lot of sense at the time but I knew it wasn't worth saying.

Mom walked around the kitchen opening drawers and cabinets, looking for who knows what.

I hooked my thumbs in my hip pockets and leaned against the wall. I wondered what would happen if Carrie didn't call today or tomorrow, or next week or next month. I wondered if I was supposed to stay phoneless for the rest of my life. I let out a long sigh. I don't know where it came from or how it got past my lips, but it filled every corner of the room.

Mom spun around. "I'm so sorry if this is interfering with your social life. But we're all going to have to make some sacrifices—and that includes you."

"Okay, okay, I'll stay off the phone." I grabbed my jacket and headed for the door. "I'm going over to Lisa's house."

"Oh no, you're not. You're not going anywhere."

"Why not?"

"It's a school night."

"Mom, it's Sunday afternoon."

"And you have school tomorrow." Our eyes locked, and my jaw fell open. "There are going to be a lot of changes made around here," she continued. "To start with, there will be no going out on a school night, and you will be in by 9:00 on weekends. That means Fridays and Saturdays only."

I was breathing through my mouth, short hard puffs that stung the back of my throat.

"And you don't go anywhere, *anywhere*, unless I know where you're going, who you'll be with, and what time you'll be home."

"But that's not fair! Carrie's the one who ran away, and I'm the one being punished for it."

"This isn't a punishment."

Well, you sure fooled me, I thought.

"It's discipline. I've been letting you and Carrie get away with too much for too long, but that's going to change starting right now."

28

She crossed her arms over her chest and stood so straight that she looked a couple of inches taller. "I believe you have to do a book report *and* a social studies project."

"But they're not due until Friday," I said.

"And exactly when do you expect to do them, Thursday night?"

"I'll start after supper. And I'll have plenty of time to finish them during the week since I'm not allowed out."

Mom's nostrils flared, and her eyes narrowed. "You'll start them *now*," she said, and then she turned on her heel and walked away.

I crumbled my jacket into a ball and threw it on the chair. I couldn't believe she was doing this to me! Every privilege I'd accumulated in my 13 years was suddenly wiped out.

And it was all because of Carrie.

Five

I was probably the only student at Franklin Junior High who was glad it was Monday morning. I hadn't spent an entire weekend in the house since I had the flu last January. And even then I got to take a trip to the doctor.

The sky was still a pearly gray when my alarm went off. I had set it an hour earlier than usual so I'd have time to do something with my hair. I hadn't touched it since Saturday and it was as stiff as cardboard when I got up. I jumped in the shower and washed it with Mom's "dry or damaged hair formula" shampoo, and then I toweled it dry and fluffed it with my fingers. And you know what? It didn't look that bad.

Mom was sitting at the kitchen table staring into a cup of coffee when I walked in. She grabbed the lapels of her bathrobe and clutched them closely to her chest as if I'd created a cold draft.

"Aren't you going to work today?" I asked as I sat across from her.

She shook her head. "I'm taking a leave-of-absence until..." Her eyes fell on the newspaper next to her cup, and then she turned the paper around and pushed it toward me.

Carrie's picture was on the front page of the morning paper. MISSING, it screamed in big bold letters. Then it said, HAVE YOU SEEN THIS GIRL? The question slammed against my heart, making it pound back in defense. I knew Carrie was missing, but there was something about seeing it in black and white, something about having it captured in print that made it really real to me. Carrie wasn't upstairs, and she wasn't coming down for breakfast. I didn't know when or *if* I'd see her again.

I tried to read the rest of the article, but the words kept swimming around on the page. I squeezed my eyes shut, and when I opened them, the tears ran down my cheeks.

Mom got up, dumped her cold coffee in the sink, and poured a fresh cup. She was too quiet for a weekday morning. I missed the click of her heels against the floor, the jingle of her bracelets when she picked up the coffee pot— all those everyday sounds you don't notice until they're gone.

"Your father's having flyers made," she said as she padded in her slippers back to her seat. "He's going to take them around to the stores and restaurants. Maybe you can help after school."

"Sure." I said. I poured some juice, swirled it around in my glass, and stared at the paper. If only I'd talked to Carrie about the party. If only I'd asked her about my hair. If only I'd said something—anything—before she walked out the door. Then maybe Carrie wouldn't have been smiling at me from the front page.

I decided to skip the bus and walk to school. It would take about a half an hour, but I had plenty of time. And I needed a chance to get Carrie out of my head.

The air was crisp and clean, and there wasn't a cloud in the sky. It was a day you'd hug if you could get your arms around it.

"Phillips! Wait up."

I knew it was David Murdock before I even looked. His voice had changed during the summer, and he sounded just like my father. He was almost 14 and lived with his grandmother in the white clapboard house I had just passed. We had an "on again, off again" friendship that had started in the first grade when I forgot my lunch and he gave me half of his peanut butter and jelly sandwich. The very next day he threw a mud ball in my face. Our relationship hadn't changed much since then.

He jumped over the porch railing and jogged toward me, his blond hair flapping against his head. "I just saw the morning paper," he said as we fell in step and headed for school.

My throat tightened. "It's a real shocker, huh?"

He laughed and said, "Not really."

I stopped. He was three steps ahead of me before he noticed. "And what's that supposed to mean?" I asked when he turned around.

"It means not really, as in I'm not really shocked your sister ran away."

"Did she tell you she was going to do it?"

"No." He moved toward me. There was egg yolk stuck in the corners of his mouth. "It just sounds like something Carrie would do."

"And what's *that* supposed to mean?"

"Aw, come on, Amy. We're talking about Carrie—Carrie, who dyed her hair green last Christmas."

"She didn't dye it green. She dyed it ash blond, and it *turned* green." I walked past him.

"And she left it that way!" he yelled from behind me.

"Only for a week!" I yelled back. "And besides, it *was* Christmas."

"That's not what you said then." He raced ahead of me, turned, and walked backward so we were facing each other again. The egg yolk was dried and cracked and sprinkled over his chin like a fine powder. He was in for a royal teasing about it when he got to school unless I told him. But I didn't.

"You called her a green-haired monster," he reminded me. "And you said she was the craziest person on the face of the earth."

"So what? She's my sister. I say a lot of things about her, but it doesn't mean I believe them." I picked up my pace and marched past him. "Carrie's my best friend."

"Then why are you always fighting with her?"

"Because we're sisters!" I walked faster, trying to shake him off but he stuck right next to me. "Look, you don't understand. You're an only child, and you don't know what it's like."

"I know when two people can't stand the sight of each other."

"You don't know anything," I screamed. "You don't even have a family!" As soon as the words were out, I wanted to stuff them back in my mouth. His parents were killed in a car accident when he was three, and he'd lived with his grandmother ever since. He said it was no big deal, that he didn't even remember his parents, but I knew he was hurting.

I could tell by the way he hung his head whenever he saw me with my parents.

I should have apologized, but I told myself he deserved it. He had no right to talk about my sister that way—no right at all.

We turned the corner, and I started to dart across the street. But he caught my arm and pulled me back. A school bus rumbled by, leaving a black cloud of exhaust in my face.

"Watch where you're going!"

"I saw it," I lied.

"Yeah, sure you did." He dropped my arm, and it slapped against my side.

"You're a real pain, Murdock."

"It takes one to know one, Phillips." We had to wait for two more buses to go by before we could cross the street. The usual groups of kids had formed around the school. David broke away from me to join his friends, and my heart turned over.

"Hey, Murdock!" I yelled.

He stopped and turned around.

"You've got egg on your face."

He spit into his hand and wiped it across his mouth. *How gross can you get?* I thought. I turned and headed for the main entrance. "Hey, Phillips!" he yelled. "I like your hair." *My hair?* I spun around, but he was gone.

Six

"AMY, I thought we were friends," Lisa said as she grabbed my arm and pulled me away from my locker.

"Huh?"

"You didn't tell me Carrie was missing! You just let me see it in the paper like everyone else!"

Wasn't there anywhere I could go to get away from Carrie?

"Do you know what it's like to have everyone think you're holding out on them?" she continued. "My parents started drilling me as soon as I got up this morning, and everyone on the bus was waiting for the inside scoop. No one believed me when I said I didn't know anything.

"You should've told me, Amy. You should've told me! I mean, maybe there was some way I could have helped." Her face was blotchy, and she looked like she was going to cry.

First it was David. Now it was Lisa. I'd gotten myself into two fights, and school hadn't even started yet.

"I'm sorry Lis, but I didn't have a chance to tell you."

"You didn't have a chance? I called you Saturday, and you said you weren't going to the party because of your hair. You said it looked like a used Brillo Pad. And look at it! It's gorgeous!"

It is? I wondered.

"Why did you lie to me, Amy?"

"I didn't!" I tried to explain it. I tried to tell her that Carrie was still in the house when she'd called. "Read the paper if you don't believe me," I said. "It's right there in black and white. Carrie was 'last seen at 2:00 Saturday afternoon.' And Mom didn't even call the police until 11:00!"

"What about yesterday? I talked to you yesterday, and you didn't say a word. Not one word!"

"I would've if my mom hadn't cut us off." I shut my locker, and as we weaved our way through the corridor, I told Lisa about Mom's new rules and regulations.

"I still think you could have told me," she

said when we reached our homeroom. "If you really wanted me to know, you would've found a way."

"I'm sorry, Lis. I really am."

She didn't answer.

That's great, I thought. The first bell rang, and I plopped down in my seat.

Lisa sat three aisles away from me, but I could still see the blotches on her face when she got to her desk.

My head started to hurt—a dull ache that spread from my eyes to the back of my neck in seconds. I rubbed my forehead, bunching the skin between my fingers. The last warning bell rang, and Sarah Jenkins slid behind her desk. She sat right across from me. I pulled some papers out of my folder and shuffled through them, acting real busy. I didn't want to look at her. What do you say to someone who had a party that bombed— *I'm sorry I missed it? Better luck next time? Oh, and by the way, who started the food fight?*

I was so busy avoiding Sarah that I didn't realize everyone else was avoiding me until second period when Miss Wilkes, our English teacher, called on me. I looked up, and everyone else looked down. I had to ask Miss Wilkes to repeat the question. Then I heard someone giggle.

I didn't make it to my next class. One of
the secretaries was waiting for me in the hall
after English. "Mr. Henderson would like to
see you in his office," she said. My heart flip-
flopped as I followed her downstairs. I'd never
been called to the principal's office before.
Carrie used to be there at least once a week—
but not me. No way!

"You can go right in," the secretary said and
left. I knocked on the door.

I heard a sound from the other side. I
sucked in my breath and turned the knob. Mr.
Henderson was sitting behind a desk that took
up most of the room. I never had liked him
much, but he'd left me alone. So, I never really
gave him much thought. Carrie couldn't stand
him, though. She said that he had the face of
a grapefruit and a personality to match.

"Amy."

I looked over my shoulder. Dad was
squished on a chair behind the door. "Did you
find Carrie?" I asked.

He shook his head.

"No, Miss Phillips," Mr. Henderson said.
His voice was a ragged wheeze. "Your sister
is still missing. But as upsetting as it is, I'm
not really surprised to hear that she ran
away."

Dad jumped up. "You keep saying that, and I don't understand what you mean."

"I'm simply referring to the fact that your daughter's behavior was a constant source of trouble from the day she entered this school until the day she left for high school."

"That's not true," Dad shot back. "Carrie had a *B* average all through junior high."

"She had a *B* minus average, Mr. Phillips. But that's not what I'm talking about. I'm referring to her conduct."

"No one ever told us there was a problem with her conduct," Dad replied.

"Oh, but we did. I met with your wife on numerous occasions, and she assured me it would be corrected. But unfortunately, it never was."

Dad shifted his weight from one foot to the other. I gnawed on my bottom lip.

No one said a word.

"Mr. Henderson," I said when I couldn't stand the silence any longer, "what am I doing here?"

Dad answered. "I want you to help me with distributing the flyers," he said. "You know all the places Carrie usually went. And I thought it would be easier if we did it together."

Mr. Henderson stood, shook hands with

Dad, and promised to have a flyer in every classroom by the end of the day.

I followed dad out to the car and climbed in. I bumped the stack of flyers that were in the middle of the seat. They toppled onto Dad's side. "Can't you be more careful?" he snapped as he straightened them out.

"I didn't see them."

"Open your eyes!"

I tried to swallow the lump in my throat, but it wouldn't budge. My neck throbbed, and my head pounded. And every time I took a breath, it felt like I was going to choke. I sucked in the air, and it came out in a sob.

Dad reached over and rubbed my shoulder. "I'm sorry, Amy. I didn't mean to yell at you. It's just that so much has happened so fast that I'm ready to explode."

I cried harder.

"Amy, please don't cry. I never know what to say to you when you cry."

"I—can't—help it." My chest was heaving, and I couldn't string my words together. "Everyone's—picking on me—and yelling at me. And—Lisa won't talk to me. I didn't even—*do* anything."

Dad was right. He didn't know what to say. He opened the glove box and handed me a box of tissues. I blew my nose, wiped my eyes, and cried some more. We just sat there until I was finished. Then he started the car, and we headed for the mall. I clutched a wad of tissues in one hand and picked up one of the flyers with the other. It was really just a blow-up of the piece that was in the newspaper— but these words were even bigger and bolder, and Carrie's picture was so clear that you could see the chip in her front tooth.

"Did you get these copied in the office?" I asked, setting the flyer on my lap. Dad works for an advertising firm that does promotional flyers and ads for agencies and businesses and anyone else who wants to call attention to themselves.

He nodded. "Everyone wanted to help. I couldn't believe how kind and generous they all were." His face softened, and he smiled.

I wondered how it felt to have friends like that.

We hit every store and restaurant in the mall, and cornered every family-run business in town. By 5:00, my feet were aching more than my head was.

"I don't think I can do this anymore," I groaned, snapping my seat belt on for the hundredth time.

"Just one more stop," he said.

I cringed. "You said that an hour ago."

"I know, but I promise this is it for today."
He drove a couple of blocks, turned right, and
parked in front of a Sherwin-Williams store.

"Dad, Carrie went to a lot of weird places,
but I don't think she ever hung out at the paint
store."

"You never know," he said with a wink. I
stayed in the car while he went in with a flyer
and came out with two gallons of white paint.

"So, did you finally give in about the living
room?" I teased.

"Honey, right now I'd do anything to make
your mother happy—anything at all."

* * * * *

"How can you even *think* about painting the
living room at a time like this?" Mom asked
as soon as she saw the paint cans.

Dad's face fell.

"But Mom, I thought you hated the color."

"That doesn't matter now!" Her eyes darted
between Dad and me. "Carrie is missing, and
all you two can think about is paint."

"Forget it," Dad said. "I'll put the cans in
the basement, and they can stay there until
they rust."

"Fine!" she yelled.

"Fine!" he yelled back.

I used to think that problems brought families closer together, that every harsh blow reinforced the seams and tied each member to the other. But my family didn't have any seams. They just had perforated edges.

And Carrie was ripping us apart.

Seven

THANKS to Dad and me, Carrie's picture was pasted all over town. And thanks to Mr. Henderson, it was pasted all over school, too. Every time I turned around, I ran into her picture.

I didn't see her face this much when she was at home, I thought as I dropped some books off at my locker before lunch.

"Basketball sign-ups are this Friday," Lisa said, arriving at her locker just as I finished at mine. She had avoided me all morning, so I thought she was talking to someone else.

"Amy," she said when I turned away, "are you signing up, or what?"

I hugged my books so tightly that the corners jabbed my ribs. "I don't know yet. I haven't really thought about it."

"We're going to have a great team this year," she said, shutting her locker and juggling her books until they all fell into place. "I've been practicing my foul shots, and I think I finally have the hang of it."

Lisa loved basketball. She was the only girl I knew who could name every team in the NBA.

"I'll think about it, but I'm not sure my mom will even let me out of the house."

She lowered her eyes.

I picked at a piece of dried-up chocolate that was stuck to the edge of my science book.

It was one of those awkward moments when the past catches up to the present, and you're stuck holding your breath.

"I'm sorry about yesterday," she finally said. "I shouldn't have given you such a hard time." Her shoulders went up and down in an I-don't-know-how-to-explain shrug, and her face got all blotchy again.

"Lis."

She looked up.

"Let's eat."

We joined Marsha Wilson at our usual spot in the cafeteria. "What is this stuff?" Marsha asked, poking at a solid white glob on her plate.

Lisa rolled her eyes. "It's rice, you ninny."

"Are you sure?"

We all stabbed our globs with our forks and

held them up for closer inspection. I flicked a piece off with my finger and tasted it. "It's rice, all right."

Lisa smiled. "I told you so."

Marsha wrinkled her face. "It's a good thing they didn't have this stuff at the country club, or our heads would have been split open."

I had forgotten all about the party and the country club. "So, who started the food fight?" I asked.

"Lester McFadden." Lisa answered.

"Lester McFadden? He's in high school."

"I know," Marsha said. "But his father works with Sarah's father, and you know how *those* things are."

I nodded. I didn't really know how *those* things were, but I nodded, anyway. I was starting to feel good again, and I didn't want to ruin it by saying something dumb.

"I knew we were in trouble the moment I saw him," Marsha continued.

"Me, too," Lisa said. "You should've seen him, Amy. He was wearing a cruddy T-shirt and jeans, and he looked like he hadn't taken a bath in a week."

"So? He always looks like that."

Marsha dropped her fork. "Amy, wake up! You don't go to the country club looking like that."

My eyes burned. Sometimes, no matter how hard I tried, dumb things slipped out anyway.

"They should've stopped him at the door," Lisa said. "They never should've let him in."

Marsha agreed.

I asked them how the fight got started. They looked at each other and shrugged. Then Lisa said, "Ask David Murdock. He was right in the middle of it."

Even though Lisa was talking to me again, it wasn't easy getting through the rest of the day. It wasn't easy getting through any day since Carrie left. Every minute seemed like an hour. Every hour seemed like a day. And every day seemed like an eternity. Time was dragging its feet. And to top it off, I still hadn't said a word to Sarah, and there were a lot of kids who still hadn't said a word to me. I felt like I had some kind of contagious disease or something. By the time the final bell rang, I couldn't stand it anymore.

"They just don't know what to say to you," Lisa explained when I saw her after our last class. "They're afraid they're going to say something dumb, so they don't say anything at all. It's safer that way."

"But how long is it going to last?"

"I don't know. I guess until they realize

you're still you."

"And how are they going to do that if they're not talking to me?"

Lisa sighed. "Is this what they mean by a vicious circle?"

"I don't know. But if it isn't, it should be." We stopped at our lockers. "You've got to help me, Lis," I said as I stuffed some books in and pulled others out. "My parents are driving me crazy. When they're not fighting with each other, they're fighting with me. And if I can't even talk to the kids around here—"

"I've got it!" she squealed. "Let's go to Sammy's." Sammy's was *the* place to go after school. It was part restaurant, serving burgers and fries and shakes, and part newsstand, with magazines and newspapers and candy. And Sammy's had an old-fashioned soda fountain that served the best hot fudge sundaes in town. All the high school kids went there. And if you were lucky—if you were *really* lucky—some of them even talked to you.

Carrie had practically lived at Sammy's. "It's perfect!" Lisa said, her eyes as wide as swimming pools. "Once everyone sees you at Sammy's, they'll know things haven't really changed."

It *was* a great idea. And I really wanted to go, but I could still hear Mom rattling off her

50

new list of rules.

I slammed my locker door and slumped against it. "I can't go."

"Amy, you *have* to go. It's your only hope. You have to show everyone you haven't changed."

"But my mom will kill me! I can't even go to the bathroom without telling her."

"So, call her."

I straightened up. "Lis, you may be on to something here. She said not to go anywhere *unless* I tell her where I'm going, who I'll be with, and what time I'll be home."

"And if you call her from Sammy's and tell her that you're there, that you're with me, and that you'll be home in an hour to an hour and a half tops—"

"—there won't be any problem," I finished for her. "Right!"

It seemed so simple.

Eight

IT was a dull gray afternoon with just enough wind to make you shiver—football weather.

Sammy's was on a corner, three blocks from school and three blocks in the opposite direction of my house. As we walked there, I practiced what I was going to say to Mom.

Lisa listened and said, "I don't know what you're so nervous about. Your mom is really nice."

"That was my old mom, Lis. The one who used to go to work every morning and tell funny stories about her boss at supper. I swear Carrie had that mom stuffed in her backpack when she left. And this new mom took her place."

I kicked a rock out of my way. It landed in front of Lisa, and she kicked it into the street.

"Has Carrie called or anything?" she asked.

It was the first time she had asked me

about Carrie, and I was glad she did. Lisa liked Carrie and I knew she'd never say anything bad about her. Sometimes I wanted to talk about Carrie without someone jumping down my throat.

I shook my head. "Not yet."

"I bet she got married," she said, her voice soft and dreamy. "I bet she met some rich guy, maybe even a prince, and they eloped."

"Carrie doesn't know any rich guys. And how would she meet a prince around here? And besides, she's only 15."

"She could've lied about her age. She could pass for 18—no sweat."

She could? I asked myself.

"I bet she's sailing somewhere in the Caribbean right now."

Sometimes, being with Lisa was like being in never-never land.

Carrie's picture was plastered on Sammy's front door. The place was semi-packed (which was normal for a Tuesday) and someone was using the phone (which was normal for any day). And everyone had their own ideas about where Carrie was.

Walter, "the Grouch," Powers swore ("may lightening strike") that Carrie was in Hollywood trying out for a movie. And Bill, "the Stick," Baker knew ("I'm telling you, this is a fact") that she was in New York, rubbing elbows with Donald Trump.

"Who's Donald Trump?" Lisa asked me as we made our way through the crowd.

"He's some millionaire who owns New York."

"Wow!"

Oh, brother, I thought.

Sam (of Sammy's) was the only one with both his feet on the ground. "She just needs some time to herself," he said as Lisa and I squeezed into a corner booth. "Another couple of days, and she'll be back in here, needling me about her picture being on the door."

"I hope so," I said.

He gave me one of his you-can-bet-on-it smiles and pulled a pad and a stub of pencil from his apron pocket. "Now," he said, "you girls look mighty hungry to me. All that reading, writing, and arithmetic can sure work up an appetite. How about some burgers, fries, and chocolate shakes—on the house." He wrote as he talked, and he didn't wait for an answer. When he was finished, he just walked away.

"Can you believe this?" Lisa asked, bouncing around on her seat. "The high school guys are actually talking to you, and we're getting free food. Amy, you're a celebrity!"

I didn't feel like a celebrity. There was an empty spot inside of me. Being in Sammy's was like being in Carrie's room—no matter how much I saw, no matter how much I heard, there was still something missing.

I looked past Lisa, and I could picture Carrie, standing at the magazine rack right next to the "this is not a library" sign, thumbing through all the latest issues until Sam pulled them out of her hand. She'd call him a tyrant, and he'd call her a delinquent. The first time I heard them, my heart froze, but then I saw the way they smiled at each other, and I knew it was just a game they played.

Carrie was like that.

And so was Sam.

"The phone, the phone!" Lisa shrieked. I looked over and saw that the pay phone was finally free. I sprinted over to it and dialed my home number.

Mom answered on the first ring.

"Mom?"

"Carrie?"

"No, Mom. It's Amy."

"Amy, where *are* you?"

"I'm at Sammy's."

"Sammy's!"

"Yeah, I'm here with Lisa, and I'll be home in an hour and a half or sooner."

"Amy, you get out of there this instant!"

"But we're just going to get something to eat."

"Are you listening to me? I want you out of there now. That place is nothing but a hangout."

"But Carrie came here all the time, and you never said anything to her about it."

"That's exactly what I mean. I don't intend to make the same mistake with you."

"But—"

"Amy, if you're not home in 10 minutes, I'm coming down there and dragging you out."

"You wouldn't."

"Try me."

I tried not to let the tears come. It felt as if there were knives digging through my throat and chest. There's nothing more painful than trying not to cry. "Mom, pleeease let me stay."

"Be home in 10 minutes, Amy."

"But it'll take me longer than that to walk home."

"Then I'll come for you."

"No!" The tears slid down my cheeks. "I'll leave right now." I hung up and wiped my eyes, but the wetness wouldn't go away.

David Murdock was sitting in my seat when I got back to the booth. He slid over to make room for me.

"Don't bother," I said. "I'm leaving."

"Hey, I can take a hint," he said and started to get up.

"This has nothing to do with you! Just give me my books."

"She won't let you stay?" Lisa asked.

"She said no way."

"But what about the food?"

I looked at David. "This is your lucky day," I said, grabbing my books from his hands. "You're about to get a free meal."

I had to walk sideways to get through the crowd. Faces were swimming through my tears, and I wanted to scream at them to get out of my way. If my mom showed up at Sammy's, I'd crawl into a hole and die.

The wind had picked up, slapping my face as soon as I opened the door. I walked so fast that it felt like my hips were pulling out of their sockets, but I had to get away as fast as I could. I didn't want anyone to see me crying.

"Phillips, wait up!"

It was David. I didn't stop. I didn't even slow down. The wind gusted behind me, pushing me along as if it were trying to help.

"Hey!" he yelled again.

I pretended I didn't hear him, but I could tell he was catching up. I dried my eyes on the sleeve of my jacket.

"You dropped your assignment book." He was right behind me. I turned halfway and yanked it out of his hand. "Thanks."

"Lisa told me what happened."

"Lisa has a big mouth."

"She's your best friend."

"So, she still has a big mouth."

"Don't get upset with her," he said, flipping the collar up on his faded jean jacket. "Carrie's the one—"

"Carrie has nothing to do with this!"

"She has *everything* to do with it. She's the reason you had to leave Sammy's, and she's the reason your mom made all those new rules."

I can't believe that Lisa, I thought. *She told him everything*!

"Everything you ever said about her was right, you know. She is a monster, and she is crazy."

"Right, look who's talking—Mr. Goody-Two-Shoes, himself. What about the food fight, Murdock? Why don't we talk about that?"

He groaned.

I knew that I had him there. I tried to smile, but the wind wiped it off my face.

"Lester McFadden started it," he said.

"He's the first one who actually threw food. All I did was ask him what hole he crawled out of, and he freaked out. The next thing I knew, I had a plate of spaghetti in my lap, and everyone was yelling, 'duck!'"

"When are you going to learn to keep your mouth shut?"

"I only said what everyone else was thinking. The guy's a slimeball. You know that."

He was right. Lester McFadden is a slimeball, and every time I thought about him at the party, I wanted to laugh, but then I'd think of Sarah. "Poor Sarah."

"Yeah. Poor Sarah. I wish there was some way I could make it up to her and her father. He got kicked out of the country club because of the food fight."

"He was kicked out just for that?"

"Yeah. I guess people like him don't belong there."

"That's a terrible thing to say!"

"I didn't say it. He did when I went over to his house to apologize." David stuffed his hands in his pockets and looked straight ahead. "He said he didn't belong with people who got so upset about a little food on the floor."

"A little food on the floor? The way Lisa talked, I thought it was dripping from the walls and ceiling."

"It was!"

We looked at each other and laughed. The wind wrapped around us, pulling us closer. And by the time we reached his grandmother's house, life didn't seem so bad.

We said good-bye, and then he swung around and started back down the street.

"Aren't you going home?"

"No, I have to go back to Sammy's," he said with a sheepish grin. "I kind of forgot my books." His eyes were dark blue, almost navy, and he had two of the deepest dimples I had ever seen.

Why hadn't I noticed those things before?

Part 2:
Life Without Carrie

Nine

I started *X*-ing off the days on my calendar the way I did when I was little and I was counting the days until Christmas. December 25th would be circled in red, and the other days *X*-ed in black. Every night I'd count the days in between. Only this time there wasn't any red circle, just a lot of black *X*s leading nowhere. But I kept doing it because—well, because you do things like that when you have nothing else to do.

"You should've signed up for basketball," Lisa said as we slid into our usual seats in the back of the school bus. "You should've listened to me."

It was the day before Thanksgiving—a cold, rainy day that chilled your bones.

I couldn't believe it was almost Thanksgiving. Time had gone from dragging its feet to galloping along so fast that I could hardly keep up with it. Now it was almost Thanksgiving. And Carrie was still gone.

As soon as the final bell rang, a party broke out in the halls and spilled into the bus. But I didn't feel like celebrating.

We still hadn't heard a word from Carrie, and just the thought of spending the next couple of days at home with my parents was enough to send my stomach into spasms. School was the only bright spot in my miserable life lately. After my brief visit to Sammy's, the kids started talking to me again, and I started talking to Sarah. We didn't talk about anything heavy. We just said things like "how'd you do on the math test?" and "can I borrow a piece of paper?"—things like that. I never mentioned the party, and she never mentioned Carrie. That was just fine with me.

I slouched in my seat, huddling deep in my coat. "But I hate basketball!" I yelled over the noise.

"You played last year."

"And I hated it. The practices were boring, and every time I got in a game, I prayed no one would throw the ball to me. Believe me, that's no way to live, Lis."

"Well, it beats sitting at home. What are you going to do for the next five days?"

"I'll probably read, watch TV, and count

the cracks on my ceiling."

"That sounds exciting."

"I'll send you a postcard."

The bus pulled out. Lisa stretched her neck, trying to see over the heads in front of us.

"Who are you looking for?"

"Shhh." She leaned into the aisle and then stood straight up. "David Murdock is sitting with Sarah Jenkins again," she whispered when she sat down.

"So?"

"So, this is the third day in a row. And they've been sitting together at lunch, too." She sank against the back of her seat and fluttered her eyes. "Isn't it romantic?"

"I can think of a lot of words to describe David Murdock, but romantic isn't one of them."

"That's because you practically grew up with him. You don't see him the way everyone else does. He's *sooo* cute."

He is? I wondered.

"And Sarah has had a crush on him for *sooo* long."

She has? I asked myself again.

"And I think it's *sooo* romantic the way fate brought them together."

Romance and fate had nothing to do with

it. It was guilt—pure and simple. He still felt bad about messing up Sarah's party, and he was trying to make it up to her. I wanted to tell Lisa that. I wanted to remind her of the country club and the food fight and David's part in the whole thing. But she had that dreamy never-never land look on her face, and I knew it was hopeless.

Instead, I stared out the window and watched the watery patterns of rain slide down the glass. *It's just guilt. That's all it is—isn't it?*

Mom had baked two pumpkin pies and was working on a chocolate cake when I got home from school. The kitchen had that warm spicy smell that makes you feel good inside.

"Are we having company tomorrow?" I asked as I peeled off my coat and hung it on the hook.

Her eyes sparkled, and she actually smiled. "No, it'll just be the four of us."

"What do you mean, the *four* of us?"

She just nodded.

My heart twisted. "Did you hear from Carrie?"

"Well, no," she said as she poured chocolate batter into the pans. "But Carrie loves Thanksgiving. It's one of her favorite days of the year. And I *know* she'll be here for it."

She scraped the sides of the bowl and then jiggled the pans until the batter was evenly spread.

Chocolate cake and pumpkin pie were definitely Carrie's favorites.

The spicy smells were turning sour. She opened the oven door, and a blast of hot air crossed the room, making it hard to breathe. "Can we have apple pie, too?" I asked. That was *my* favorite—apple pie with a scoop of vanilla ice cream and caramel syrup drizzled over the top.

"Oh, honey. I don't have time for that. I still have to make the stuffing. And I want to put fresh sheets on Carrie's bed." She slid the pans in the oven and turned on the timer.

I wanted to ask her why she was baking for someone who wasn't going to be there. I wanted to ask her why she was rewarding Carrie for running away. I wanted to ask her a lot of things. But I didn't.

I was afraid to hear the answers.

We always ate Thanksgiving dinner at noon. Year after year—through snow storms and rain storms and championship football games, the turkey was always on the table at the same time. It was something you could count on.

At 12:15, my mouth was watering.

At 12:30, my stomach was growling. I curled

up on the sofa and tried to concentrate on the TV, but Dad was on the recliner, clutching the remote control. He was a zapper. Every time I blinked my eyes, the channel changed.

At 12:45, Mom pushed the curtain away from the front window and peered outside.

"Mom, when are we going to eat? I'm starving."

"Let's wait 10 more minutes," Mom said.

Dad got up, walked over, and stood in back of her. "She's not coming, Elizabeth. You can wait until midnight, and she won't be here."

"Just give her 10 more minutes. That's all. I promise she'll be here."

We didn't eat until two o'clock.

By then, the turkey was tough. The stuffing was soggy. And the sweet potatoes tasted like glue. But no one said a word.

We didn't have to.

Carrie's empty seat said it all.

I couldn't sleep that night. I bounced from one side of the bed to the other, from my stomach to my back, and I even tried sleeping on the floor. But nothing worked.

So, I did what I needed to do. I went into Carrie's room and lay on her bed and hugged her doll and pretended it was her.

Ten

IT snowed a week before Christmas—big fat flakes that turned to slush as soon as they hit the street.

Dad gave me a ride to school. He used to do that a lot before Carrie left—before our lives changed. I hardly ever see him lately. He usually leaves for the office before I get up and doesn't come home until late at night. There have been days when I even forgot he was around. And sometimes I wondered if he ever forgot about me.

I watched him as he drove. He had his usual tight grip on the steering wheel, and his jaw had the same thrust of determination. But there was something different about his eyes. The lids were like heavy slabs, and the laugh lines that played around the corners had deepened into furrows. And the more I stared at him, the deeper they got.

He was turning into an old man right in front of me.

I crouched against the door, wishing I could get away, wishing that I could run backward through time, back to our white living room, and my straight hair, and a sister who drove me crazy.

I just wanted things to be the way they were.

Dad and I didn't talk much on the way to school. He asked me how school was going, if I had any tests that day, and how I liked the snow—all the usual questions parents ask when they don't know what else to say.

And I gave him the usual answers: "fine, no, it's okay." I had this weird feeling that he wanted to say more, that there was a reason behind his sudden offer of a ride to school. I found out I was right.

"Do you want to do some Christmas shopping tonight?" he asked as soon as he stopped the car. "We could leave right after supper and wipe everyone off of our list."

He made it sound so simple, so normal. "Yeah, sure," I said, "if you can clear it with Mom."

"What do you mean *clear* it?"

"Tonight's a school night. I'm not allowed out on a school night."

"Since when?" he asked.

"Since Carrie left." I told him about Mom's new list of rules, and when I was finished he said, "She can't do that. Why didn't you tell me?"

"I thought you knew."

He ran a hand through his hair and then rubbed the back of his neck. "You have to tell me these things, Amy. You have to come to me when things get out of hand."

"How can I?" I asked as I opened the car door. "You're never home."

I drifted through the day on a wave of confusion. I'd always thought of my parents as a matched set, like a pair of book ends. But I guess they're not.

Dad was living in one world, and Mom was in another. And I was lost somewhere in between.

Where do I fit in? I wondered.

It was times like this when I missed Carrie the most. Oh, we did fight a lot, but when Mom and Dad seemed to be going crazy, Carrie and I would hold on to each other.

But now when I reached out, there was no one there. I wanted Carrie to come home.

I wanted it so badly, I ached inside.

I don't know how Dad did it, but Mom had no problem with my going out on a school night. She acted like it was no big deal, like she couldn't understand why I was so shocked when she said yes.

Mothers!

The car felt like the inside of a freezer. I turned the heater on and got blasted with frigid air.

Dad turned it off. "Wait until the motor warms up," he said, and then he reached into his back pocket and pulled out his wallet. "How much money did Carrie take from you?"

I told him, and he handed me 40 dollars. "That's interest, too." he explained when I said it was too much.

We shopped for an hour and had nothing to show for it. I didn't expect to have any money, so my mind was a total blank. And every time Dad picked out something for Mom, he put it back because he wanted "something better."

"Do you have any ideas?" he asked when we crossed another store off of our list.

I ran my fingers over the 20 dollar bills in my pocket. "How about a gold chain, like the one Carrie took."

He smiled, but there was a sadness in his eyes that made the smile seem out of place.

The jewelry store was crowded. We crept along, looking in the glass cases. There were earrings and watches and bracelets that looked like they weighed a ton, and all the price tags were turned face down.

"The chains must be on the other side of the store," Dad said. I followed him across the store and ran smack into David Murdock.

"Forget it, Murdock," I teased. "You can't afford this place."

He didn't answer. He just stood there staring at me. "Will there be anything else?" a saleslady asked him.

"No," he said and handed her a bunch of money. She rang up the sale and gave him a small oblong box.

It was wrapped in silver and gold and had a miniature red bow in the middle. "I'm sure your girlfriend will love it," she said.

He mumbled something back, and then he turned to me and said, "See ya," and charged through the crowd.

Girlfriend? *Wait until Lisa hears about this*, I thought.

But I knew I'd never tell her. I'd never be able to get the words out.

"What do you think?" Dad asked when I joined him. He had a rope of silver in his hand.

"That's not the chain Mom had before."

"Honey, I bought that other chain seven years ago. I'll never find another one exactly like it," he replied.

"But this isn't even close! It isn't even the same color!"

"What difference does it make?"

He didn't understand.

No one did.

Not even me.

Eleven

CHRISTMAS day began with a flicker of excitement.

Maybe today, Carrie would come home.

Maybe today, our lives would get back to normal.

Mom had hung her hopes on our tinsel-covered tree. And even Dad had a funny look on his face. But as the hours slid by, I knew it was just another day—a day to be gotten over with.

Late in the afternoon, I made my traditional visit to Lisa's house where Christmas was in full swing. The place was bulging with family and friends. Her dad gave me a glass of punch, and her mom stuffed me with cookies. When I was finished, Lisa and I tucked ourselves into a quiet corner to exchange gifts.

I gave her a New York Knicks T-shirt to add to her NBA collection, and she gave me an oversized crewneck sweater that matched one of my skirts perfectly. When we were finished, I slipped back into my coat.

"Don't you want to hang around for a while?" she asked as we walked to the door.

It would have been nice to blend in with the crowd, to spend a few hours absorbing some Christmas cheer. But I couldn't do it. I belonged somewhere else. "Nah," I said. "I'd better go. But thanks, anyway."

When I got home, David Murdock was waiting for me in the living room. He was standing next to our tree, talking to Dad while Mom sat on the sofa wringing her hands.

As I dropped Lisa's gift on the deacon's bench, Dad said something about needing a cup of coffee. He tugged on Mom's arm, and she followed him into the kitchen.

"I think I gave your mom a heart attack," David said when they were gone.

"You probably did. But don't worry about it. She has one every time the doorbell rings." I glanced at the pile of unopened gifts under the tree—Carrie's pile—and wondered what Mom would do with them now.

"Here," David said, shoving a small oblong box in my hand. "Merry Christmas."

I stared at the silver and gold wrapping paper and the miniature red bow in the middle, and my heart started thumping.

I remembered the words the salesclerk had said, *I'm sure your girlfriend will love it.*

It wasn't for Sarah. It was for me!

"Come on, Phillips. Open it."

I tore off the paper and popped open the lid. It was a bracelet of big, thick, silver links knotted together. "Oh, David, it's beautiful."

"It's a friendship bracelet," he said, shifting his weight from one foot to the other. "I'm sorry about all the cruddy things I said about your sister, and I wanted to give you something to prove it."

I rubbed the silvery knots, and tears filled my eyes.

"Hey, look. It's no big deal. So, don't get all mushy on me."

"I'm not," I said and forced a smile. "I just feel bad because I don't have anything for you."

"Well, you *can* do me one favor."

"Name it."

"Don't tell any of the kids at school where you got it. I've got a reputation to protect."

I nodded and said, "Don't worry. I don't want anyone getting the wrong idea, either."

We talked for a few more minutes and then I walked him to the door, clutching the small box in my hand. "Thanks again."

He just shrugged.

I stood in the doorway and watched him leave. His hair was turning darker—dirty blond—and his coat made his shoulders seem really broad.

"Hey, Phillips," he said, breaking into my thoughts. "I hope your sister comes home soon."

I smiled and nodded and closed the door. No matter who I was with, no matter what I was doing, Carrie was always there, poking her way into the moment.

She had left. But she wasn't gone.

I took the bracelet out of the box and put it on. It was heavy and shiny, the kind of bracelet everyone would notice. And it was the silvery knots that I liked the best. For the first time since Carrie had left, I felt connected to someone else. *A friendship bracelet.* I wiped my eyes with the back of my hand and then rubbed the knots until my fingers ached. He actually liked me just for myself. And I knew I'd wear the bracelet everyday so I wouldn't forget.

I took a deep breath and went into the kitchen to show Mom and Dad.

"You can't keep that," Mom said as I dangled my hand in front of her.

"Yes, I can, Mom. David gave it to me out

of friendship. It's a—"

"And you're giving it right back!"

"I got a sharp pain in the pit of my stomach, and my chest was so tight that I could hardly breath. "But why?"

"Because girls your age don't accept gifts like that from boys," she explained. "It's not proper."

I tried to tell her that it was just a friendship bracelet, that it wasn't anything serious or romantic or anything else she associated with "proper." But the more I talked, the angrier she got.

"You can't keep it!" she screamed, slapping her hand on the table. "I won't allow it!"

I looked at Dad. He was holding his coffee mug so tight that the veins were popping out of his hand.

You said I should come to you. You said I should let you know when things got out of hand. Well, here I am, Dad. Do something!

He drank his coffee.

"Give it back, Amy," Mom said. Her face was on fire.

"You give it back! You explain why I can't keep it!" I screamed, unsnapping the clasp. I threw the bracelet on the table. "I hate the stupid thing, anyway!" I ran from the kitchen and up the stairs.

"I'm going to talk to his grandmother about this!" Mom yelled after me. "I'm going to let her know what her precious grandson's been up to!"

I ran into my room, slammed the door, and flung myself on the bed and cried. I cried because parents don't play fair. They don't send you a warning. They just give and take and spin you around so fast that you're too dizzy to see what's in front of you. And then when you finally find something to hold on to, something to help you keep your balance, they yank that away from you.

I cried long and hard.

I cried until I couldn't cry anymore.

Twelve

I once read that the opposite of love isn't hate. It's apathy, not caring. That's the point I wanted to reach. I didn't want to care about my sister or my parents. I wanted the freedom to just exist, to be, to stop hurting. But the heart doesn't come with buttons and switches. There's nothing to press or flick to empty its chambers. It has a mind of its own. So, you pretend. And if you're good at it, you can fool everyone into thinking you don't care. And if you're *really* good, you can even fool yourself.

January rode in on the back of a blizzard. Our Christmas vacation was extended until someone found our streets. Everyone complained about the weather, but I liked the snow. I liked the way it made everything clean and quiet, as if the world was wrapped in whispers.

I stared out the living room window and watched it pile high on the rooftops and bare trees. I watched it drift into soft curves against the cars and fences. But I wasn't just daydreaming. I was busy developing the new me.

No more pestering Mom to use the phone.
No more begging to go out.
And no more tears!

The way I figured it, if I didn't open my mouth, I wouldn't get hurt.

My thoughts blended with the snow, and I wondered how long we'd both last.

The bus was packed the fist day back to school. I slid into a backseat, and a few blocks later, David Murdock squeezed in next to me. I wanted to ask him if he got the bracelet back. I wanted to explain what happened. I wanted to tell him my mom was freaking out, and there was nothing I could do to stop it. But I couldn't say anything. There were too many kids around, too many ears. And I knew if anyone overheard us, he'd kill me. So, we talked about school and the snow and how great it would be for skiing.

When we got off the bus, he ran to catch up to Sarah, and my heart almost stopped.

Forget it, Phillips. You don't care anymore, remember? This is the new you. And no one's ever going to hurt you again.

I dumped some stuff in my locker and was heading for my homeroom when I saw Lisa hobbling down the hall on crutches. Marsha Wilson was walking beside her, carrying her books.

"Lis! What happened?"

"I tore something in my knee," she said, stopping to adjust a crutch.

"Tell her how it happened," Marsha said and then looked at me and rolled her eyes.

Lisa smiled proudly. "I was practicing my foul shots."

"In two feet of snow," Marsha added. "Can you imagine anyone being dumb enough to play basketball in two feet of snow?"

"Hey," Lisa said, defensively, "it's not my fault no one shoveled the driveway."

I helped Marsha with Lisa's books, and we listened patiently as she moaned about missing the rest of basketball season and groaned about future seasons. "What am I going to do if I can't play ball?"

Marsha suggested needlepoint.

"Needlepoint!"

"Sure, it's perfect," Marsha said with a wink. "You can even do it in the snow."

Lisa was on crutches for two weeks and drove me crazy the entire time. She'd accepted the fact that her basketball career was temporarily on hold, but she was desperate for something else to do. So, when Mr. Henderson announced plans for a school play, Lisa decided it would be perfect for both of us.

"No way," I said as we headed for class. "I'm not getting up on that stage! Besides, this play is going to be really weird."

"It's not *weird*. It's different. It's an adventure! We'll be breaking new ground and discovering new talent."

"Falling flat on our faces!"

"Oh, come on, Amy. We've got to do *something*."

"Something? Maybe. This play? Forget it." It was written by the senior high school class as part of their creative writing assignment. The home economics students were making the costumes, and the junior high students were producing it.

It was the blind leading the blind.

Mr. Henderson had called it "a joint venture, unity between the schools, and the merging of young creative minds."

Yuck!

Lisa coaxed and nagged between every class, but I didn't give in. "No way," I said over and over again.

The next day she handed me a copy of the script and said, "Auditions are next week."

"Lisa!"

"Just come with me, Amy. You don't have to audition if you don't want to. Just be there. Pleeease. I'll never ask you for another thing as long as I live. I promise."

"That's what you said last year when you talked me into playing basketball."

"I know, but this is *really* it. Cross my heart!" I stuffed the script into one of my folders and told her I'd think about it. It's not that I minded going with her—I didn't mind that at all—it was having to ask Mom for permission that made me queasy. After all, I'd be breaking my new number one rule. Don't ask for anything.

But I guess Lisa was worth it.

She would've done it for me.

Mom didn't bat an eye when I asked her. "Sure," she said. "Fine, go ahead." There was a calmness about her that was almost scary. It was as if she had given up, as if she had nothing left to fight for, as if the fire had burned out.

I took a can of soda pop up to my room and when I was finished with my homework. I sprawled on the floor and read the script.

The play was called *Buttermilk Ridge*, and

it was about a family who lost their farm because they owe the government too much money. I didn't know anything about farms, and I wasn't itching to learn, but I liked the characters. They were warm and funny and tough. They weren't the outside kind of tough. They were the inside kind—the kind that makes you fight for what you believe in, no matter how bad things get.

I read the entire script, and when I was finished, I read it again and again and again. My favorite character was Charlene, the oldest daughter. She wanted her father to stay put and stand up for his rights, and she wasn't afraid to tell him. She was the kind of person you'd want for a friend—a real fighter—someone who would stick by you, someone you could count on.

I liked her.

I liked her a lot.

Thirteen

THE auditorium was jammed the day of auditions. But it wasn't because everyone had a sudden case of acting fever. It was because all the English teachers had offered extra credits for anyone who participated.

"Incentive," they called it.

Bribery, I thought.

I sat with Lisa and listened while Mr. Williams, the high school drama coach, explained the play. He talked about plot and structure and characterization while everyone squirmed in their seats. Then he said that anyone who was just interested in helping with scenery or lighting or just wanted to be "extras" could leave. The auditorium cleared out.

I started to get up but Lisa pulled me back. "You promised to stay with me," she said. I slouched back down in my seat.

There was a bunch of high school kids sitting in the first row. Mr. Williams introduced them as "some of the authors" and said they would make the final casting decisions. "And I will have the privilege of being your director," he added with a dramatic bow.

Someone applauded.

Lisa was trying out for the part of Mrs. Brubaker, a friendly neighbor who was always stumbling over her own feet. It was a small part, but she had some good lines, and it was the kind of character everyone would remember. The only problem was it was the last part to be casted.

"Lisa, we're going to be here forever," I groaned after Mr. Williams announced the order of characters.

"Yeah," Lisa said. "Isn't it great? We get to watch everyone else!"

Yeah, Lis. It's really great, I thought.

Eight girls tried out for the part of the mother. I yawned through the whole thing.

The father's part went a lot faster. Only three guys tried out. And one of them was David Murdock. After him, I didn't think they needed to look any further. With his voice, he had to get the part.

The part of Charlene was next. I perked up. Ten girls stood in line for what I considered to be *the* part, and they were all doing it wrong!

"They're whining," I whispered to Lisa. "Those are strong lines, and they're whining like little kids!"

"Shhh!"

I crossed my arms over my chest and gritted my teeth. By the time the last girl got onstage, I couldn't stand it anymore.

"Charlene's a fighter, and they're turning her into a wimp!"

She jabbed me with her elbow. "Will you be quiet!"

"I studied the script, Lis. They're not doing it right."

"Shhh!"

I tried to sink into my seat and take deep breaths and do all the things they tell you to do to relax, but the anger was bubbling inside of me.

As soon as Mr. Williams thanked all the girls for auditioning, I grabbed my script and marched onstage. There was some mumbling from the front row, but Mr. Williams shushed them and told me to "give it a try."

I started reading from the script, but after the first few lines, I didn't need to use it. I was no longer Amy Phillips. I was Charlene— feisty, determined Charlene. I screamed and yelled and did everything I pictured Charlene doing when I had read the play.

When I was finished, Mr. Williams applauded.

*   *   *   *   *

"We did it, Amy! We did it! We got the parts!" Lisa was bouncing up and down so much, I was afraid she'd wreck her knee again, but it didn't seem to bother her.

Our names were posted on the bulletin board. Lisa was Mrs. Brubaker, and I was Charlene. And David Murdock was going to be my father. *That's just great,* I thought.

I didn't even want to be in the stupid play, but having my name matched to Charlene's made my insides tingle.

I did it. I really did.

Opening night was eight weeks away, and rehearsals were three times a week.

When I told Mom and Dad, they gave me their "that's nice" smiles and promised to be there on opening night.

Lisa and I practiced our lines every chance we got. And the first time I rehearsed with David, my heart raced. All I could think about was that friendship bracelet.

When we were finished, I cornered him

88

backstage. He deserved an explanation or an apology, but when I explained what had happened, he said he didn't know what I was talking about.

"Didn't you gét the bracelet back?"

"No."

"Then your grandmother must have it."

He shook his head. "No, she would've said something. We're like this," he said, crossing his fingers.

"Then where is it?" My voice cracked. If my mom wasn't going to let me keep the bracelet, then she should've returned it. David could've gotten his money back, or have given it to someone else like Sarah. I rubbed my wrist. It was bare, but I could still feel those beautiful silvery knots. They were locked in my mind.

"Hey, don't worry about it," he said and placed his hand on my shoulder. "I told you, it was no big deal. It probably would've turned your wrist green, anyway."

"I'll ask her about it," I said. "If she still has it, I'll get it and give it back to you."

"No! You'll only get her upset. And then maybe she won't let you be in the play. Just forget it. It'll show up again someday."

I didn't want to listen to him. I wanted to stand up to my mom the way Charlene would've done. But David was right. One wrong word, and I'd be sent crawling back to my room.

I was a wimp.

Mondays, Wednesdays, and Thursdays were my favorite days of the week. Those were the days we had play rehearsals. I lived for them. Every time I got onstage, I yelled a little louder, cried a little harder, and when I walked off, I felt 10 pounds lighter. Being someone else was so much easier. I knew exactly what to say, and what was going to be said back. And I knew how the story would end. I was living in a different world, and I loved it.

Halfway through rehearsals, Mr. Williams pulled me aside and asked who my drama coach was.

"Huh?"

"Your drama coach," he repeated and crouched to my level. "Who's teaching you how to act?"

"No one." My hands were getting clammy.

"You mean this is just natural talent?"

I hated questions I didn't understand.

"I don't know, Mr. Williams. I—I'm just trying to be Charlene."

He grabbed my shoulders and squeezed so hard that I thought my bones were going to snap. "Amy, I can't wait until you get to high school. You're going to be fantastic!"

I am?

Mr. Williams hovered over me all the time. He taught me how to tone down and how to combine a gesture with a word for a more dramatic effect. And while Lisa and David teased me constantly, I loved every minute of his attention. By the time we had our dress rehearsal, Charlene was real.

I couldn't wait until Mom and Dad saw me onstage.

Fourteen

"I can't be there tonight, Amy," Mom said, rolling a chunk of ground meat between her hands and then dropping it into a film of hot oil.

"But you promised," I said, slamming my books on the kitchen table. "It's opening night."

"I know, and I'm sorry." The frying pan hissed and spat as she added another meatball. "Your father will be there, but both of us can't go."

"Why not?"

She didn't answer. She just stood there, her back to me, her hands working with another chunk of meat as if making perfectly round meatballs, in the exact same size, was the most important job in the world.

"Answer me, Mom! Why can't you both be there?"

"You know why," she said, tossing the words over her shoulder.

"Carrie." Every time I said her name, part of it stuck in my throat.

"She's going to come home, Amy. I know it. And I have to be here when she does."

"It's been five months! When are you going to stop waiting for Carrie?"

"Never!" She spun around so fast that she almost lost her balance. "I'll wait five months, five years. It doesn't matter. I'll never stop waiting. She's my daughter!"

"So am I!"

I ran from the kitchen, up the stairs, and threw myself on my bed. Carrie took more than my earrings, and Mom's chain, and Dad's jersey, and the money. She took pieces of our lives, pieces she had no right to, pieces that could never be returned or replaced. And I hated her for it.

"Amy, I'm sorry. I really am." Mom said, walking into my room.

I squeezed my eyes shut.

She sat on the edge of my bed.

I turned my head away.

"Please, try to understand," she continued. "Carrie may be trying to get up the courage to call or come home. And if no one's here when she does, she may never try again."

She sighed and shifted her weight on the bed.

I didn't make a move. I could see a giant dustball in the corner of my room. Carrie used to say that you didn't have to vacuum a floor because if you waited long enough, all the dirt, dust, and loose hairs would find each other and form a ball. Then all you had to do was pick up the ball and throw it away. And it worked too—as long as we found the balls before Mom did.

My throat started to ache, and I dug my fingers into the bedspread. I couldn't swallow.

"Amy, please say something."

"I HATE HER. I hate her. I hate her. I hate her."

She pulled me into her arms, but everything inside me was screaming and yelling. I pushed her away and buried my face in the pillow.

"She hurt you." Her voice was all cracked and broken. "She hurt all of us. But I believe she's going to come home. I have to. Otherwise, there's nothing left."

I didn't hear her leave, but I could tell she was gone by the emptiness around me.

Otherwise, there's nothing left.

What about me? Didn't I count at all? At that moment, I hated Mom, too—hated her for loving Carrie.

* * * * *

I kept telling myself that Mom would change her mind, that at the last minute she'd throw on her coat and come with us, that she wouldn't let me down.

But only Dad was in the audience opening night. Once I was onstage, none of that mattered. I stepped out of my life and into Charlene's. There was only her and her story, and for a short time, life was so much better.

Backstage after the play, David gave me a big bear hug, and I hugged him back.

We didn't say anything.

We didn't have to.

It would've been the perfect way to end the day, if Lisa hadn't seen us.

"What was that all about?" she asked after David left.

"Nothing," I said in my most innocent voice, but she didn't believe me.

"You're holding out on me, Amy. There's something going on between the two of you, and I'm going to drive you crazy until I find out what it is."

"Lis, I don't have time to talk about it now. My dad's waiting for me, and I still have to get changed and get all this makeup off."

"Then I'll call you later," she said, backing away. "And I don't care what your mom says. I'm getting to the bottom of this tonight."

* * * * *

"You were really great tonight, honey," Dad said for the 10th time as we slid into a booth at Pizza Circus.

It felt funny being there with just him. It always had been the four of us stopping in for pizza—after movies and piano recitals and shopping trips. We'd laugh and talk and argue about the toppings. I wondered if it would ever be that way again.

We quickly agreed on a small pepperoni pizza and two large sodas. And after the waitress left, I looked at Dad. He was staring out the window and turning his wedding ring around on his finger.

When I was little, he used to carry me up the stairs on his back. "Drop me on my bed," I'd say, twisting my arms around his neck.

"Drop you on your head?"

"No! On my *bed*."

"Oh, your *bed*." And we'd both laugh. *Why does life have to change?*

The waitress came back with our sodas.

"Mr. Williams says I have a lot of natural talent," I said, poking the ice with my straw.

"That's great! You were really good tonight, Amy. It's too bad Mom wasn't there."

Why wasn't she? And where's Carrie? And why did she leave? And what's happening to all of us? The questions flew through my mind, but I didn't ask them. I couldn't. What if he didn't have the answers? What then?

I squeezed my eyes shut as the tears formed behind them, burning there with anger and pain, and a feeling of helplessness that I couldn't understand.

"Your mother does love you, Amy." I opened my eyes, and he held me in his.

"Does she?"

"Yes, she loves you very much. And so do I. We're all grieving..."

"Carrie's not dead," I shot back. "She can't be."

"Grief doesn't only come with death, Amy. It's there whenever we suffer a loss. And we've all lost Carrie. We keep hoping she'll come home, but we don't know if she will. All we know is she's gone, and we're all handling it in our own way.

"Your mother finds comfort in sitting by the phone. I find it in my work. You found it in the play. For you to punish her for not being here tonight would be the same as her punishing you for not staying at home. We can't tell someone else how to grieve, anymore than we can tell them how to feel. It takes time, honey, and patience—with ourselves and each other. And even when the pain goes away, part of us will still be waiting."

"But I'm tired of waiting, Dad. I don't want to do it anymore. I want it to be finished. I want to be happy again."

He reached into his pocket and pulled out a sparkling lump of silver. "Will this help?" he asked, picking up one end and dangling it in front of me.

"David's bracelet! *You* had it?"

"No," he said, shaking his head. "Well, not exactly. I convinced your mom to think it over before she did anything. She put it in her jewelry box and didn't say another word about it until today. She gave it to me before we left the house and told me to give it to you after the play." He took my hand and dropped the bracelet in my palm. My fingers curled around it.

"I'm sorry, Amy. We let you down, and I'm sorry. I'm sorry for both of us."

I don't think I ever loved anyone as much as I loved him at that moment.

Fifteen

MOM was curled up on the sofa thumbing through a magazine when we got home. "How was the play?" she asked, jumping to her feet.

"It was fine," I said.

"It was fantastic," Dad gushed. "It was absolutely fantastic. And Amy was the star."

"Da-ad."

"You were, honey. You were the best one on that stage. And you know it. I was so proud of you." He leaned over and kissed the top of my head. "You should've seen her up there, Elizabeth. You should've—"

"Tomorrow," she blurted. The word hung in the air. I wanted to reach out and grab it and show it to her and ask her what it meant. But I knew once I moved, it would be gone. "There *is* another performance tomorrow, isn't there?" she asked.

I nodded slowly.

"Good," she said. Her eyes darted nervously around the room as if she was looking for her next line. Then she said, "How about some hot chocolate?"

"Not for me," Dad said. "Too much pizza."

"How about you, Amy? Hot chocolate with marshmallows? It's your favorite." She looked like she was going to cry.

My stomach was so full that it felt like it had a lump of lead in it. And every few minutes, the taste of pepperoni tickled the back of my throat, but I said, "Sure." I'd been living in Carrie's shadow for so long, I wasn't about to pass up a minute of special attention.

Dad went upstairs to find some antacid, and Mom and I went into the kitchen. She started heating some milk on the stove while I sat at the table playing with a napkin. Every time I moved my hand, the bracelet slid around my wrist. I dropped the napkin and rubbed the silvery knots.

Mom turned and leaned against the counter. "It's a beautiful bracelet," she said as she watched me rub my fingers raw. "You're lucky to have a friend like David."

"Yeah, I am." I slid my hand off the table and put it in my lap. Mom was so unpredictable, so moody. I was afraid she'd change her mind and snatch it away from me again.

"I'm sorry I took it from you, Amy. It's just that I was so angry at Carrie for not being here for Chirstmas. And then, when I saw the bracelet, I got so scared."

"Why?"

"Because I didn't realize you and David were that close. And I didn't want you to have any secrets from me. When I saw that bracelet, I knew you were growing up and changing. And I was so afraid that one day I'd turn around and you'd be gone, too.

"I thought if I took the bracelet, I could keep you. I thought that you'd stay my little girl, and that you wouldn't go away."

I put my hand back on the table. "I'm not going anywhere, Mom."

"I know." She poured some chocolate into a mug then added the milk and stirred. "It was a stupid idea. I've known that for a while. I was waiting for the right time to give it back. Then, when I decided not to go to the play, I thought it was the perfect way to make it up to you. Only I didn't know what to say. And you were so angry at me."

"So you gave it to Dad."

"Yeah," she said, dropping a handful of marshmallows into the mug.

I thought as long as you had the bracelet

back, nothing else would matter. But I was wrong. I should have been in that audience tonight." She placed the mug in front of me. Tears streamed down her cheeks. "I'm sorry, Amy."

"Are you really coming to the play tomorrow?" I asked and held my breath.

"Yes," she said with a tremor in her voice. "I promise."

I promise. I'd heard those words before, but this time I believed her. This time I thought she really meant it.

I sipped on the hot chocolate.

It had never tasted so good.

She asked about the play, and I told her about the plot and the characters and how Mr. Williams thought I had "natural talent." I felt like I had my mother back again.

"Oh, honey, that's wonderful. You must've been great. I—I should've been there," she said, and another tear ran down her cheek.

"Tomorrow," I said.

"Definitely," she said.

The phone rang and she jumped, and then she sagged back to her normal position. "That's Lisa," she said. "She's called twice already. I told her you'd call her tomorrow, but she said it was urgent."

"I'm sorry, Mom. I told her—"

"It's okay," she said, cutting me off. "From now on everything's going to be okay." Then she smiled and said she was going to bed. "But don't stay on the phone too long," she added as she walked through the dining room. "It's getting late."

The phone rang again and again, and I couldn't figure out what to tell Lisa. How could I explain David when I didn't understand him myself? How could I explain what was going on when there wasn't anything going on?

Just tell her the truth, I thought as I grabbed the receiver.

"Hello."

"Amy?"

"Yeah."

"Amy...it's Carrie."

Part 3:
Love is a Four-Letter Word

Sixteen

WHAT do you say to a sister who you haven't talked to in five months? *It's nice of you to call? What's new? How have you been?*

I didn't say anything. I yelled for Mom, and as soon as I heard her on the phone upstairs, I hung up.

My hands were shaking.

I sat at the table and stared at the gooey clump of marshmallows floating around in my mug. My mind was a total blank. It was as if the play and David and the bracelet had never happened, as if Carrie had magically wiped them out so only she could exist.

She had called from a runaway shelter to say she was all right and wanted to come home. And that call sent Mom flying to the front door where she paced for days on end, missing every performance of the play.

"You promised!" I screamed at Mom over and over again. "You said you'd definitely be there. You promised!"

She never answered.

She couldn't.

She was too busy waiting.

Great timing, Carrie.

But it wasn't until four weeks later, on a Wednesday night—smack in the middle of my favorite TV show—that Carrie finally stepped back into our lives.

Poof, she was gone.

Poof, she was back.

It was one of those moments that you dream about for so long, you can taste it. But then, when it actually happens, it's nothing like you imagined.

Mom and Dad were all over her the minute she appeared. They were all laughing and crying. I'd never heard Dad cry before, and I wanted to join them. I really did. But everything inside me was twisting and turning, and I couldn't straighten it out.

Carrie looked so different. Her hair was a dozen shades lighter, and she was wearing so much makeup, she looked like *she* belonged onstage. I sank a little deeper into the recliner and stared at the TV.

I never thought she'd look different. I never

thought she'd change.

Carrie broke away from Mom and Dad.

"Amy." Even her voice was different.

I stood up automatically, and when I looked into her eyes, my heart turned over. They weren't Carrie's eyes. These were all cloudy and used as if they had seen too much and couldn't handle anymore. If it wasn't for the familiar lopsided grin playing around her mouth, I would've sworn it wasn't her.

Except for an occasional heaving sound from Mom, there was absolute silence. We just stood there facing each other—sisters and strangers.

Finally, I asked the question I had wanted to ask for so long, "Why?"

The word seemed to bounce off the walls, and Mom made a funny kind of noise. But Carrie didn't answer. Her grin disappeared, and there was a hardness in her face I'd never seen before.

"Answer me, Carrie. Why did you leave?"

"Amy, please, we don't have to get into that right now," Mom said, moving closer to my sister. "There'll be plenty of time—"

"Will there?" I asked, fighting back the tears. "How do you know she'll still be here in the morning?" I didn't wait for an answer. I ran upstairs to my room, slamming the door shut behind me.

Their voices slipped through the walls, and while I couldn't hear exactly what they were saying, I knew they were talking about me, about how I ruined everything. But I didn't care. None of it seemed real.

This was supposed to be one of the happiest moments in my life. That's how I had dreamed it. So, why did I feel all battered and bruised?

I lay on my bed, my pillow locked in my arms, and let the tears fall. Maybe all the good feelings were buried underneath.

A little while later, Carrie knocked on my door. "Amy, can I come in?"

I wanted to tell her to go away and never come back, but I was afraid she would, so I said, "Yeah," and sat up.

She walked in, stood in front of me, and stretched out her hand. "I just wanted to return these."

My mother-of-pearl earrings—the ones that disappeared along with Carrie, the ones I thought I'd never see again—were sitting in her palm.

"Go on—take them. They're yours." I held out my hand, she tilted hers, and the earrings tumbled back to me.

"What happened?" I asked, squeezing my

hand shut. "Couldn't you get enough money for them?"

"That's not why I took them." She backed up, and I thought I saw her bottom lip tremble. "I just wanted to make sure you knew I was gone."

I wanted to say something, but all the words were jammed in my throat.

Carrie walked away.

I tossed and turned most of the night, trying to find a pocket of sleep to fall into. But every time I slid inside, Carrie's words echoed through the darkness, and my eyes popped open.

"I just wanted to make sure you knew I was gone." What was that supposed to mean? Didn't she know how much I loved her, how much I *used* to love her?

Why did she have to change?

Seventeen

"I think you owe your sister an apology." My brain was still scrambled from the night before, and it took a few seconds for Mom's words to get through. She was propped against the kitchen counter, her terry cloth robe cinched around her middle.

If I didn't get much sleep, she didn't get any. The bags under her eyes were so big, you could have stuffed groceries in them.

I pulled out a chair and was lowering myself into it when her message sunk in. "*I* owe *her* an apology? You've got to be kidding!"

"You were rude and arrogant, and Carrie was very upset."

Poor Carrie, I thought.

I glanced over at Dad. He was flawlessly dressed in a three-piece suit, studying the front page of the morning paper. He looked like he had fallen asleep the minute his head had hit the pillow.

Carrie was the only one missing, as usual. "I want you to apologize before you leave for school."

"No." I reached for the carton of orange juice. It felt too warm to be any good but I poured some, anyway.

"Amy—"

"No!"

"Peter."

We both looked at Dad. He was turning to page two. Sometimes I thought the whole world could explode, and he'd simply turn another page of the newspaper. "You better eat breakfast and get moving," he said, looking up and over the paper, "or you'll be late for school."

I sipped my juice and locked eyes with Mom. She was giving me one of her you're-not-going-to-get-away-with-this looks, and I was ready to tell her to save it for Carrie when I noticed the gold chain around her neck.

I almost choked.

It was the one Dad had given her for their 10th anniversary, the one that disappeared along with my earrings the day Carrie left. I wanted to ask her about it. I wanted to know exactly what Carrie had said when she returned it.

But I couldn't.

I didn't want her to know I cared.

Mom walked over to the stove and slammed the frying pan onto the burner. "Eggs or French toast?" she asked, her back stiff, her shoulder blades sticking out like wings.

"I'm not hungry." I pushed away from the table, deliberately scraping the chair across the floor.

Mom spun around. "You apologize to your sister before you leave this house."

"I don't have anything to apologize for!" I grabbed my books and left.

I stopped at the drugstore, bought a candy bar and a can of pop, and found Dad waiting in the parking lot when I came out.

"Come on!" he yelled out the car window. "I'll give you a lift."

I ripped open the candy, took a bite and chewed so hard that my teeth hurt.

"It's going to be kind of hard to eat and drink and juggle all those books at the same time."

Good point. I got in the car, dumped my books on the floor, and popped open the soda.

"That was some surprise last night," he said as we pulled out of the parking lot.

I bit off another piece of candy and turned the radio on. He turned it off.

"Your mom's really scared, Amy."

"Of what? Carrie's back all safe and sound. She should be walking on air."

"It's not that simple," he said, tightening his grip on the steering wheel. "She's afraid it won't last. She's afraid Carrie will leave again. That's why she was so bent on your apologizing. She doesn't want her to have a reason to leave."

"She didn't have a reason the first time, did she?" I asked.

He shrugged.

"You didn't ask her?"

"No," he answered.

"But you're going to, right?"

He sighed.

"This whole thing stinks! She disappears for months, drives us all crazy, and no one says a word!"

"That's not true, Amy!"

"Isn't it?"

"This doesn't concern you!" He slammed on the brakes, and my seatbelt tugged against my shoulder. A truck the size of New Jersey had stopped in front of us. Another inch, and we would have made the evening news.

I got my books and jumped out of the car. "Amy, get back in here."

"I'd rather walk!" I said, slamming the car

door in his face.

I knew I'd be late for school, but I didn't care. I didn't care about anything anymore—except the pain that was splitting me in two.

Part of me wanted to crawl back into my childhood where Mom and Dad could fix all the hurts, and Carrie was someone I knew.

And the other part wanted to race into the future where life had to be a lot clearer and saner, and I could look back at all this and finally understand.

If I could flip a coin, it wouldn't matter which part of me won, as long as it didn't land on its edge, as long as I could be anywhere but here.

Eighteen

I had to stop in the school office for a late slip—I'd never had to do that before—and on the way out, I tore Carrie's picture off the bulletin board. Someone had blackened out her front teeth.

I was dying to talk to Lisa, but she was absent. "She has strep throat," Marsha told me between classes. "I called her last night, and she could hardly talk."

Great.

I could've told Marsha that Carrie was back. I could've told my entire class, and I would've had enough attention to last me a lifetime. But I didn't trust my words with anyone but Lisa. Not yet, not now.

I was antsy all day. It felt like there was someone jumping around inside of me trying to get out. I didn't want to be in school, and I didn't want to be at home.

I didn't want to be anywhere.

By the time the final bell rang, I'd decided to walk home because I needed the time to think, and walking took longer than riding the bus.

David was waiting for me at my locker. He started talking about how warm it was getting, and how he couldn't wait until the end of the school year, and about the spring dance that was still four weeks away.

But all I could think about was Carrie and my parents and what was happening to all of us. And David was stumbling over his words so much that I couldn't tell where one sentence stopped and another began.

"So, what do you think?" he asked as I closed my locker.

"About what?" My eyes must have been as foggy as my mind because he just looked at me and shook his head and said, "Forget it," and walked away.

What was he talking about? I ran after him. "Come on, Murdock. Give me a break. I wasn't listening."

"Thanks, Phillips. That really makes me feel better."

"I'm sorry."

"Yeah, sure you are." He was walking so fast that I could hardly keep up with him.

"Carrie came home."

He slowed down. "When?"

"Last night."

"That's great," he said half-heartedly as we pushed open the front doors.

"No, it isn't. I thought it would be, but it isn't. It isn't great at all." I told him all the gory details as we walked home. I told him about my fight with Carrie and Mom and Dad. I told him about how much Carrie had changed and how I dreaded going home. "That's why I wasn't listening to you. I was too busy wondering what was going to happen next. I'm sorry."

He shrugged it off. "That's okay," he said. But it wasn't.

I owed him a lot. Oh, we had our share of fights, and there were times when I wanted to strangle him. But he always seemed to be there when I needed someone the most. And I let him down—not just now, but a couple of weeks ago, too.

I had told Lisa about the bracelet—after I'd told him I wouldn't tell any of the kids. I didn't want to tell her. I mean, it wasn't like I planned it or anything. It's just that she was bugging me about him so much, and I was so happy to get the bracelet back. But I made her promise ("Cross your heart and hope to die") not to tell anyone else.

I trusted Lisa, the way David had trusted me, the way I had trusted Mom, the way Mom had trusted Carrie.

"So, do you want to go to the dance or not?"

"Huh?"

"Look, Phillips. I'm not going to beg. This is the *last* time I'm asking—so listen up. Do you want to go to the spring dance with me? Yes or no?"

The dance! That's what he had been talking about. He wanted to go to the dance with me.

Me!

Every nerve in my body tingled and then died. I wasn't the person he thought I was.

"Yes or no?" he repeated through clenched teeth.

"I told Lisa about the bracelet."

"What?"

"The bracelet," I said, shaking my wrist in front of him. "I told Lisa after I said I wouldn't tell anyone. I went back on my word."

"What are you trying to tell me, Phillips— that you're not perfect? Well, I've got news for you. I've known that for a long time, but that still doesn't answer my question."

"You mean you still want to go to the dance with me?"

He nodded. "Yeah, so what do you say?"

What do I say? "Okay, sure, that would be great." I sounded like an idiot. I looked at him, and he was smiling. But I had to turn away. My cheeks were getting hot.

When I got home, I went straight to my room and locked the door. I didn't want anyone—not Carrie, not anyone—to ruin what I was feeling inside. So, I lay on my bed and stared into space and thought about the dance and David and how lucky I was to know him.

I stayed in that cloud of happiness until Mom called me for supper.

Nineteen

W E took our usual places at the kitchen table and looked like the perfect American family—Mom, Dad, and the two kids. All we needed was the dog, and we could've been a Norman Rockwell painting.

"I guess I should have made something a little more special," Mom said, passing the meatloaf to me.

There was total silence. She could have served mud, and no one would have noticed. I slid a piece of meat off the platter and handed it to Carrie.

Mom tried another topic. "Amy was in the school play this year."

"I'm sure she gave an Oscar-winning performance." I caught the sting in Carrie's words, but it bounced right off of Mom.

She laughed and said, "Well, she was really good."

I had to hook my feet around the legs of the chair to keep from falling off. "Mom, you weren't even there."

She flinched.

Dad stabbed at a piece of meat and shoved it in his mouth.

Carrie said, "You haven't changed a bit, have you, Mom? You're still trying to make everyone believe you're the perfect mother."

"I don't know what you're talking about."

"Don't you?"

Mom grabbed the gravy boat and drowned her potatoes. I closed my eyes.

"You know," Carrie said, "I used to think you were really fantastic. Every time I made a mistake, you were right there to sweep it away. It was great. I could do anything I wanted, and you were right there to protect me. I really thought you loved me.

"Then I realized it wasn't me you were protecting. It was yourself, your image as the perfect mother. Only I kept messing things up. You couldn't exist with a daughter like me. But that was easy to fix, wasn't it, Mom? All you had to do was pretend I was someone else."

"That's not true!"

"Isn't it? What about the time I got picked up for shoplifting?"

My eyes shot open.

Dad's fork fell from his hand, clinked against the edge of his plate, and landed on the floor. "What shoplifting?"

"It was nothing, Peter."

"Mom, they caught me with the stuff in my pockets."

"They dropped the charges."

"After you paid the bill."

"What was I supposed to do, let them send you to jail?"

"What shoplifting?" Dad asked a little louder.

Carrie ignored him and said to Mom, "You were supposed to help me! You were supposed to love me enough to tell me I was wrong. But you couldn't do that, could you? Even when I tried to talk to you about it, you pushed me away. 'Don't worry about it,' you said. 'It was just a big mistake.' Yeah, it was a big mistake, Mom, just like me."

Dad's fist hit the table, and we all jumped. It sounded like a bomb going off. "What shoplifting? I didn't know anything about this!"

"Of course, not," Mom shot back at him. "Every time something went wrong in this house, you ran to your office. The only way I could get you to stay home was to pretend everything was okay."

Dad lurched forward. The veins in his neck were sticking out like ropes. "So, this is all my fault! Is that it?"

The accusations shot back and forth, each person trying to outdo the other. I pushed the food around on my plate until it all disappeared in a teary blur. Carrie was unraveling everything, peeling away all the layers I needed to believe in, and I was scared there'd be nothing left.

"STOP IT!" I screamed.

They all looked at me as if I'd just stepped into the room. I looked at Carrie. "Why is everything their fault? What about you? You know right from wrong, but every time you get in trouble, you look for someone else to blame. You haven't changed a bit either, have you, Carrie?"

Carrie's mouth twisted into two thin lines, and her eyes narrowed into slits. But I didn't back down. "If things are so rotten around here, why did you bother coming back?"

"Amy!" Mom sounded like she was going into shock, but I didn't look at her.

The lines in Carrie's face cracked and crumbled, and I saw the wetness in her eyes. She stood, stumbled around the table, and stopped next to me. "At least you've got the guts to tell the truth."

Mom buried her face in her hands. Dad turned sideways and stared at the wall. No one said a word.

*   *   *   *   *

There used to be an oak tree right outside my bedroom window. When I was little and scared, I'd scrunch into a ball on my windowsill and pretend it was there to protect me. Its limbs were giant arms, ready to scoop me up and carry me away to a land of sunshine and roses.

I don't fit on that window sill anymore. And last year, Dad chopped the tree down. "It's too close to the house," he had said after it was hit by lightning.

I missed that tree.

But sometimes, when I tried real hard, I could still see it standing there. At least no one could take that away from me.

I didn't bother turning on a light. I just sat on the floor, leaned against the side of my bed, and asked myself questions I couldn't ask anyone else.

What happens to all of the dreams that don't come true? Do they just wither and die? Or, do they keep piling up inside of you until your heart breaks?

What happens when people aren't who you want them to be? Do you love them, anyway? Or, do you just throw them away like yesterday's garbage?

My parents weren't perfect, but neither was I. David had made that quite clear, but he liked me, anyway.

And Carrie—well, Carrie was Carrie. She was unpredictable, rebellious, a royal pain in the neck. But she's the only sister I have.

I heard Mom and Dad come upstairs. Their voices rose and fell like waves, and then they disappeared behind their bedroom door.

A little while later, Carrie came in. I didn't hear her walk in, but I knew she was there. She had that kind of presence. She walked around the side of my bed and sat next to me on the floor. Moonlight pooled at our feet. And somewhere, deep inside, I knew this was all I ever wanted, just to have Carrie next to me again.

But how long would it last? Another day? A week?

"Are you going to stay?" I asked, my voice shaking and my heart pounding."

She pulled her knees up to her chest and tucked them under her chin. "Would it matter?"

Carrie was a part of my life. Maybe she wasn't the best part, but she was a *real* part, a part I didn't want to lose again.

"Yeah," I said, pulling my knees up to match hers. "It would matter."

She made a loud sniffling noise, and her face glistened with tears.

"Carrie?"

"As long as it matters," she said, staring straight ahead. "As long as someone cares."

Maybe loving someone isn't enough.

Maybe they have to know it.

About the Author

Janet Dagon's dream when she was young was to become a nurse. After she graduated from college, she worked as a nurse in a hospital. Then she left to become a full-time mother. It wasn't until after she had her youngest son that she began to write professionally. She has written and published articles in magazines, but fiction is her first love.

Janet gets most of her ideas for her books and short stories by asking the question, "what if...." The idea for *MISSING: Carrie Phillips, Age 15,* came to Janet when she was watching a television report about runaways. A teenage girl was reunited with her parents and younger sister after she had disappeared for over a year. Janet kept wondering what it was like to have your sister run away. Janet then wrote "Waiting for Carrie," which first appeared in a magazine as a short story. That short story grew into this novel.

Janet lives in Pottsville, Pennsylvania, with her husband David and her three sons, Mark, Jeff, and Scott. When she's not writing, she enjoys reading, needlepoint, taking long walks, board games, and people watching.